THE
HAPPINESS

by

DAVID GRIFFIN

with drawings by

LESLIE GREENER

MEDIA MASTERS
SINGAPORE

Written at Changi in December, 1942.
Produced by:
The Education Centre,
AIF POW Camp,
Changi, Singapore.

Buried in Changi Prison before Christmas 1942
Dug up from its secret hiding place
after the liberation of Singapore on September 5, 1945

Published in Singapore, 1991
by
MEDIA MASTERS PTE LTD
34 Genting Lane, #02-06 Kheng Seng Bldg., Singapore 1334. Tel: 749-2703, Fax: 744-5032

Printed by Grenadier Press.

ISBN 981-00-2654-4

To the children
whose fathers went to Singapore
and never came back.

EXPLANATION OF THE CHI CHAK

We all know what a monkey is, and all of us have seen a frog. But some of us have never met a Chi Chak. He is a wise little lizard from the jungles of Malaya. He is a friendly little fellow, too, who often makes his home in the houses of Malayan people. He is called a Chi Chak because that is what he says as he runs happily about the walls and ceilings of their rooms.

ONCE upon a time there was a Chi Chak, a Monkey and a Frog, who all lived together in a little house deep in the middle of the jungle.

The Chi Chak's name was Winston and he was very clever.

The Monkey's name was Martin, and he looked after the house and did the cooking.

The Frog's name was Wobbley, and he worked in the garden.

Every morning after breakfast Winston used to climb the very highest tree in the jungle to set his wind trap. He was so clever that he had been able to think of the wind trap out of his own head. He set it at the top of the very highest tree and he was able to catch wind in it.

If a North Wind was blowing, Winston would first of all catch it in his trap; then he would tie the wind up in a banana leaf and carry it home for lunch. But if a South Wind was blowing they would eat it for dinner, because the South Wind tasted better.

Old Wobbley worked all day in his garden growing rice and vegetables, which he carried back to the little house in a small black bag with a silver lock on it.

After Winston and Wobbley had set
out each morning, Martin would make the
beds and sweep out the house, and then
he would go to the larder to see what
they could eat for lunch.

In the larder there was a big bin that
Wobbley always kept full of rice, and
there was a small bin with fruit and vegetables in it.   Also there were four bags
into which Winston put the winds he had
caught in his wind trap.

Now, if the bag for the North Wind was all blown out like a baby's cheeks, Martin knew that they could have boiled North Wind for lunch, and he would decide to cook it very nicely for Winston and Wobbley.

But this clever wind trap of Winston's was the only one in all the jungle, and every morning hundreds of creatures came to the back door and asked Martin for a few puffs of wind for their lunch too.

Martin was such a dear old Monkey that he never said "No" to anything and so, by the time every jungle creature had been given a puff of wind, there was never any left to cook for Winston and Wobbley.

Then Martin would give a sigh, because he, too, was very fond of boiled North Wind, and he was not very fond of rice and vegetables.

One day Winston and old Wobbley came back to the little house deep in the middle of the jungle. Winston gave his banana leaf full of wind to Martin, and old Wobbley went to the larder and emptied his rice and vegetables into the bins.

When they sat down to lunch, Martin gave them each a plate of plain rice and vegetables, without any wind at all. Winston said, "Where is the boiled North Wind I trapped yesterday?" and Martin hung his head and answered in a sad voice, "The jungle people came to the back door and asked for some wind and I gave it all away."

Then old Wobbley, who had a very funny deep voice, said, "Never mind, Martin, I will grow plenty of rice and vegetables," and Winston said, "It does not matter, Martin, I will trap more wind." And they all laughed and were very happy.

NOW next day old Wobbley was digging in his rice field and suddenly his spade uncovered a strange wooden box. He scraped away the mud and saw that the box was fastened with three big brass pins. The box was very heavy and old Wobbley could only just lift it. But he would not open it without his friends.

At mid-day, when his work was done, old Wobbley hopped away to the little house. The big box was on his back and the small black bag with the vegetables in it was on the top of the box, and he looked like a van piled with furniture.

As soon as he reached home old Wobbley put the wooden box on the lunch table, and when the others saw it they became very excited.

Martin cried out, "Quick! Let us open it up and see what is inside!"

But Winston, who was very clever, said, "No, do not touch it. It may be bewitched. We are very happy in our little house and we have everything we want. We do not need the thing that is in the box."

Then Martin looked sad and said, "Oh, Winston, couldn't we have just one look? We have everything in the world, but there are many creatures who have not. The box may be full of treasures which we could give to our neighbours."

Winston nodded his head thoughtfully but he did not say anything. Then suddenly old Wobbley said in his funny deep voice:

"Let us go and ask the three wisest creatures in the jungle!"

"That is a good idea, Wobbley," said Winston. "Lock up the house, Martin, and we will be off."

So the three happy friends set off through the jungle. Martin swung himself along the branches of the tall trees and old Wobbley hopped over the ground with Winston clinging to his back.

The first place they came to was a great black swamp, guarded by glow worms, who whizzed about in chariots drawn by giant mosquitoes. The swamp was the home of Dreamy Bill, the oldest and wisest tortoise in the world. He was fast asleep when they arrived at his house, but Martin woke him up by tapping on his shell with a pick handle which was put there on purpose.

When at last Dreamy Bill poked out his head, Winston told him about the wooden box that old Wobbley had found, and asked him if they should open it.

"It is no good asking me questions," said Dreamy Bill, shutting one eye. "I gave up thinking over a hundred years ago. You had better ask Flappy; he knows most things." Having said this, he quickly drew his head back under his shell, and they heard his muffled voice saying, "Please go away and don't move the pick handle."

So Winston, Martin and Wobbley continued their journey in search of Flappy, the wise king of the birds.

Flappy lived at the mouth of a huge dark cave in the heart of the jungle mountains. As they drew near the cave they saw thousands of fierce birds wheeling and falling through the air, and crying out in horrible voices, "King Flappy, king of all birds! Three strangers are here!"

Old Wobbley looked at their cruel beaks and hard eyes and began to tremble, but Winston cried out, "King Flappy, king of all birds, we come for advice."

And Flappy, who was smoking a pipe, waved his right wing and said in rather a fussy voice, "Oh, very well, very well, but hurry, whatever you do, hurry."

So Winston, Martin and Wobbley ran to the cave and in a few words told Flappy about the wooden box which Wobbley had found when he was digging in the garden, and asked his advice.

Flappy thought hard for a few minutes. He had to light his pipe five times because each time he had an idea his pipe went out. At last he said: "I have no more tobacco for my pipe so I cannot think any more thoughts. You must go and consult the Bumble Bee, for he knows everything."

Then Winston, Martin and Wobbley said good-bye to Flappy and thanked him very much, and ran out of his cave as fast as they could.

And as they left the cave they heard the fierce birds crying, "O, King Flappy, king of all birds! The strangers who came to seek your advice are gone!"

Presently Winston, Martin and old Wobbley came to the beautiful kingdom of the Bumble Bee. Spreading beneath the trees was a field of flowers. The flowers were of every colour—red, purple, yellow and gold—and the field was surrounded by a wall of rainbows.

In the middle of the field there was a great scarlet flower as big as a house, and in the middle of the flower sat Bumble, the Bee who knew everything.

Bumble listened very carefully to Winston, Martin and Wobbley when they told him about the wooden box, which Wobbley had found in his rice field. He put his head on one side and sat still for a long, long time. Then, after he had thought and thought and thought, he said in a voice which sounded like a whistle and a buzz, "Return to your little house and open the wooden box, for in it you will find the happiness of the world."

LESLIE GREENER

Now Slinky, the wicked snake of the jungle, who did not like people to be happy, had been listening, and when Bumble said these words, Slinky called out, "Do not listen to old Bumble! He knows nothing. Give me the wooden box and I will build you a house of diamonds and pearls finer than a king's palace!"

But Winston, Martin and Wobbley paid no attention because they loved their little house much better than any king's palace, and Bumble only smiled. So Slinky knew that his deceitful plan had failed and he slipped away into the long grass, hissing angrily.

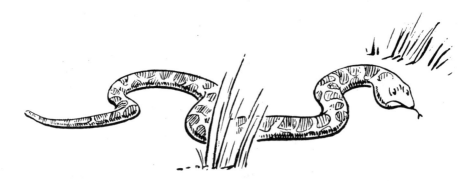

THEN Winston, Martin and Wobbley
thanked Bumble for telling them what
to do and hurried back home to the little
house deep in the middle of the jungle.
There was the wooden box standing on
the table, exactly where they had left it.

As Martin was the strongest, he climbed
on the box and undid the three brass pins.
Winston and Wobbley held their breath
while Martin flung open the lid.

The box was lined on the inside with
rich blue velvet, and in it were three books!

There was a tiny book with Winston written on it, a medium-sized one with Wobbley written on it, and a very large one with Martin written on it.

"Look! Look!" cried Martin. "The big book has my name on it!"

"And the next biggest has my name on!" cried Wobbley.

"And my name is on the littlest," said Winston, "because I am the smallest!"

Each of the friends lifted out his book with the greatest care, and on the bottom of the box was printed in letters of gold:

"In these three books there lies the secret of happiness. Read them; then go out into the world and teach your fellow creatures how to be happy."

So Winston sat down and began to read his book, and Martin and Wobbley began to read theirs too.

When they had all finished reading their books, old Wobbley said to Winston:

"What secret did you learn from your book?"

And Winston replied, "My book says that the world will be happy if people learn to be clever, and if they learn to be like Martin and old Wobbley."

And old Wobbley said, "My book says that the world will be happy if people work hard and if they learn to be like Martin and Winston."

And Martin said, "My book says that the world will be happy if people are generous and kind and if they learn to be like Winston and old Wobbley."

At first they did not understand what the books really meant.

Then Winston, who was very clever, said, "I will tell you what they mean. They mean that we three must go out into the world and teach our neighbours how to be clever, industrious and kind, so that they can all be as happy as we."

So ever since that day, Winston the Chi Chak, Martin the Monkey and old Wobbley the Frog leave home every morning and go out to teach the world the lesson of happiness.

But, when the shadows fall, they come back to the little house deep in the middle of the jungle. On warm evenings you can often see Winston on the wall, explaining his wind trap to his friends; if you are lucky, you may catch a glimpse of Martin swinging through the trees with his book under his arm; and, after you have gone to bed, you may sometimes hear Wobbley's funny voice, which sounds to other children like er-urr . . . er-urr . . . er-urr . . .

But, if you hear that sound, you will know that he is telling some of the other frogs how one day, many years ago, when he was digging rice for his two friends, Winston and Martin, he found the wooden box with the magic Books of Happiness. And you can be quite sure that when he is talking about those days, the kind old fellow will be smiling.

THE END